Written by Sue Graves
Illustrated by Jan Smith (Advocate)
Designed by Blue Sunflower Creative

Language consultant: Betty Root

This is a Parragon Publishing book
This edition published in 2003

Parragon Publishing
Queen Street House
4 Queen Street
Bath, BA1 1HE, UK

ISBN 1-40542-704-3
Printed in China

The Apple Picking Party

p

Notes for Parents

Reading with your child is
an enjoyable and
rewarding experience.
These **Gold Stars** reading
books encourage and
support children who are
learning to read.

The **Gold Stars** reading books are filled with fun stories,
familiar vocabulary and amusing pictures. Sharing these
books with your child will ensure that reading is fun. It is
important, at this early stage, for children to enjoy reading
and succeed. Success creates confidence.

Starting to read

Start by reading the book aloud to your child, taking time
to talk about the pictures. This will help your child to see
that pictures often give clues about the story.

Over a period of time, try to read the same book several times so that your child becomes familiar with the story and the words and phrases. Gradually, your child will want to read the book aloud with you. It helps to run your finger under the words as you say them.

Occasionally, stop and encourage your child to continue reading aloud without you. Join in again when your child needs help. This is the next step towards helping your child become an independent reader.

Finally, your child will be ready to read alone. Listen carefully to your child and give plenty of praise. Remember to make reading an enjoyable experience.

Using your Gold Stars stickers

You can use the **Gold Stars** stickers at the back of the book as a reward for effort as well as achievement. Learning to read is an exciting challenge for every child.

Remember these four important stages:

- Read the story **to** your child.
- Read the story **with** your child.
- Encourage your child to read **to you**.
- Listen to your child read **alone**.

Jack was looking forward to school today.
It was Sports Day. He had practiced for the
races all week.

He had practiced running and hopping and skipping. He had even practiced the three-legged race. Best of all, he had practiced for the sack race. Jack always won that!

But this morning it was raining. Jack and his friends ran to school. He ran past the farm. Farmer Frank saw him.

"Be careful you don't slip, Jack," said Farmer Frank. "I slipped on the wet grass and hurt my leg. Now I can't pick all my apples."

When Jack got to school, Mrs. Smart, Jack's teacher, had some bad news.

"I'm afraid it is too wet for Sports Day," she said.

The sports field was full of big puddles.

"You can't run on such a wet field," said
Mrs. Smart. "You might slip."

The children were very sad.

Jack told Mrs. Smart about Farmer Frank.
"He slipped and hurt his leg," said Jack.
"Now he can't pick all his apples."

Then, Mrs. Smart had an idea.

She phoned Farmer Frank.

"We will help you pick your apples," said
Mrs. Smart. "We will come to the farm when
the rain stops."

That afternoon, the rain stopped. Mrs. Smart and the children went to Farmer Frank's farm. They took lots of things with them.

They took bags. They took buckets. They took baskets. Jack even took sacks.

"Here we are to pick your apples," said Mrs. Smart.

Mrs. Smart and Farmer Frank's wife picked the apples from the trees. There were lots and lots of apples to pick.

"Phew! This is hard work," said Mrs. Smart.

Farmer Frank and the children put the
apples into the bags. They put apples into
the buckets. They put apples into the
baskets. They even put apples in Jack's sacks.

The children took the apples to the barn.
There were apples everywhere! Soon they
packed them in boxes.

Farmer Frank's wife gave everyone a cold drink. Mrs. Smart and the children told Farmer Frank about their wet sports field.

"It was too wet to have our Sports Day," said Mrs. Smart.

"I wanted to run in the sack race," said Jack, sadly. "I love that race."

21

Just then, Farmer Frank had an idea.

"Let's have an Apple Picking Party in the barn," said Farmer Frank.

"What's an Apple Picking Party?" asked Jack.

"Wait and see," said Farmer Frank.

The Apple Picking Party was a lot of fun. First of all, there were lots of races. The children ran and jumped. They hopped and skipped. Farmer Frank won the three-legged race on his own!

APPLE
PICKING
PARTY

There was even a sack race.

Jack won it easily!

Everyone clapped and cheered.

Then, Farmer Frank's wife gave them all party food. There were sandwiches. There were cakes. There were pitchers of lemonade. Best of all, there were apple pies and ice cream.

"Thank you for picking my apples," said Farmer Frank.

"Thank you for our Apple Picking Party," said Jack and the other children.

Answer these questions. Look back in the book to find the answers.

Why was there no Sports Day?

What did Farmer Frank have to get into the barn?

Why did Farmer Frank need help?

What did the children carry the apples in?

What did Farmer Frank call the party?

Who won the
sack race?

Now retell the story in your own words.

Gold Stars reading books are for children who are beginning to read.

- Familiar, repeated vocabulary
- Short sentences
- Large, clear type
- Pictures that support the text
- Review activity